Peter Pan

ONCE UPON A TIME IN LONDON, THERE LIVED a little girl whose name was Wendy. She lived with her parents and her two brothers, John and Michael. Wendy had a very vivid imagination, and every evening before they went to sleep, she would tell them a story.

One evening the children's parents went out. Wendy, John, and Michael were already asleep, so they didn't notice when the window opened and the bedroom curtains parted gently to admit a strange young boy into the room. He looked about him keenly and seemed to be searching for something.

"There it is, Tinker Bell! It slid under the chest of drawers!"
said the boy to a strange little golden light that hovered nearby.
It was. in fact, a beautiful little fairy. Then the boy knocked
over a chair and Wendy awoke with a start just as the
fairy slipped into a drawer to hide.

"Who are you?" Wendy asked.

"My name is Peter Pan," replied the boy, still
looking under the chest of drawers.

"I'm looking for my shadow. It's run away again!"

"Well then, we'll have to sew it on!" said Wendy,
jumping out of bed to fetch a needle and thread.

"How did you get in here?" she asked her
new friend, as she began sewing his shadow
onto his foot.

"Well, I just flew to the window and opened it," Peter Pan replied, simply.

As Wendy did not seem to believe a word he was telling her, Peter Pan explained some more:

"I live in Never Never Land with the Lost Boys. They are children who fell out of their baby carriages when they were tiny. Come with me to Never Never Land," Peter Pan begged her. "The Lost Boys need a mother so badly!"

"But I can't leave my brothers all alone!"

"Well, they can come with us," replied Peter Pan, happily.

Peter Pan taught Wendy, John, and Michael to fly. And, when everyone was ready, they took off into the clouds with Tinker Bell the fairy. How they enjoyed racing the birds and sliding down the rainbows!

Past the second star on
the right and then straight
on till morning: that was the way Peter
Pan and his new friends went, until
Never Never Land appeared on the
horizon. No sooner had they landed than a
crowd of children threw themselves upon them,
laughing! They were all dressed in bearskins that made them
so fluffy and roly-poly that it was impossible to catch them.
Wendy thought she would be squashed flat and even Peter
Pan found it very difficult to call them to order.

"Listen everybody, I've brought you a mother! We are
going to take her to our cave and you are going to behave
very well for her."

To enter the Lost Boys' cave, the
children had to crawl inside a hollow
tree trunk, then let themselves slide down at top
speed until they dropped into the middle of their
underground home.

Wendy, John, and Michael soon got used to their
new life. Wendy was kept busy looking after the
children, doing the washing, and mending their
clothes. She made sure they were in bed by seven
o'clock every evening and told them all a story
before they fell asleep.

One day, when Peter Pan and Wendy had taken the boys to the mermaids' lagoon, the sky suddenly grew dark and they saw a great ship appear. The captain, draped in a voluminous black cape, looked most sinister. He was giving orders to his ship's mate, who was tying up a beautiful dark-haired girl.

"Tie her up tight and attach stones to her ankles. She must not be able to float. She must drown!"

"It's Captain Hook,"
explained Peter Pan to Wendy,
who was clinging on to him as tightly
as possible.

"Look! He has a hook instead of his right hand. That's because
I cut off his hand in a duel and threw it to the crocodile!"

Wendy was terrified.

"He has captured Tiger Lily, the Indian Chief's daughter! We must save her!"
cried Peter Pan, thrilled at the thought of confronting his enemy once more.

In the twinkling of an eye, he had flown to the boat and was taunting
the pirate Captain:

"So, Captain, have we made this trip for our health?"

Mad with rage, Captain Hook turned round. The ship's mate took fright, jumped into the water and disappeared. Peter Pan grabbed Captain Hook and took him to a rock that was as slippery as soap. The fight was unequal, the boy kept dodging here and there, attacking from all sides, while Captain Hook made the air around him whistle as he slashed about with his terrible iron hook, without ever hitting his adversary. Suddenly, the Captain slipped and fell into the water. Then a tick-tock sound could be heard coming nearer and nearer. Captain Hook had another mortal enemy apart from Peter Pan—the crocodile who had swallowed his hand after the duel … and had swallowed his watch with it! Captain Hook let out a yell and swam off as fast as he could.

Peter Pan ran to free Tiger Lily, the Indian Chief's daughter. They were welcomed as heroes when they took her back to her father's camp, where the Indians lived. Sitting round the fire, they smoked the peace pipe.

Later, in their underground house, Wendy put the children to bed and hugged them. Michael asked her:

"Tell me, Wendy, are you really our mother now?"

Wendy quickly realized that Michael would soon have forgotten his real parents and that they needed to return to London. When she told Peter, he refused to go with them.

"Go to London with you? Of course not! I am not going to risk growing up at any price!"

Wendy understood that only those who lived in Never Never Land remained children forever.

It was very sad to say goodbye.

They were about to leave the cave, when they heard a terrible roaring outside. Furious at his defeat, Captain Hook had launched an attack on the Indian camp. The children could not get away until the battle was over. The Indians agreed that if they won, they would beat their tom-toms to signal that the way was clear.

The brave Indians fought like lions but, taken by surprise, they were defeated by the treacherous pirates. Captain Hook had won, but this victory was not enough for him, he was really after Peter Pan and his band. But how could he flush them out of their underground house?

Then Captain Hook played a mean trick, he ordered the Indians to beat their tom-toms. Inside the cave, there was a great whoop of joy:

"The tom-toms! An Indian victory!" shouted Peter Pan and the children.

Believing the way was clear, John went out first. One of the pirates grabbed him, tied him up in a sack, and threw him into the ship's hold. Next, they caught Michael and Wendy. Tinker Bell was captured using a butterfly net. Not one of the prisoners had time to call out and warn Peter Pan.

Quaking with terror, the three children were tied to the ship's great mast and Tinker Bell was locked in a birdcage. Gloating with triumph, Captain Hook was thrilled at the thought of throwing them all to the crocodile, but he decided to put off the execution until the morning.

While the Captain slept, Tinker Bell
managed to escape from her cage
and flew as quickly as she could
to warn Peter Pan. The boy did not hesitate for a
moment, but rushed to help his friends. When he
arrived aboard the pirate ship, all was quiet and the only
sound that could be heard was the tick-tock of the crocodile circling the ship,
confident that a fine feast was being made ready for him.

As soon as they saw him arrive, the children recognized Peter Pan. But he
signaled them to be quiet and set them free in silence: he wanted to surprise
Captain Hook in his sleep. He crept softly toward the Captain's cabin,
opened the door and yelled loudly:

"This time, Captain, it's you or me!"

Captain Hook jumped out of bed, but Peter Pan hit him hard in the right spot and he doubled over. Woken by the noise, the pirates had started to struggle with John and Michael. But the two boys had had time to steal their weapons from them and their victory was quick and easy. So Captain Hook and Peter Pan were left alone, face to face, for a final duel.

"Young upstart," cried Captain Hook, "your last hour has come!"

"No, you villain," replied the boy, "you had better look out for yourself!"

Their swords clashed during a long exchange. Little by little, Peter Pan pushed the Captain to the edge of the ship, finally forcing him up against the railings.

"Push him over, Peter! Push him over!" shouted the children.

Peter Pan gave a little kick and toppled Captain Hook overboard where he fell straight into the jaws of the waiting crocodile.

Then Peter Pan ordered the ship to set sail for London. Exhausted by the battle, Wendy, John, and Michael fell asleep on the bridge and remembered nothing of the return journey. When the sun rose on London the next day, they were far from Never Never Land, safely back in their little beds and, when they woke up, it was already time to get up for school.

THE END

Tom Thumb

ONCE UPON A TIME, THERE WAS A WOODCUTTER and his wife who lived in a little house near a forest. They loved each other dearly and wanted for nothing. Nevertheless, they were unhappy because they had no children. One evening, the wife said to her husband:

"Ah! If only we could have a child, just one! Even a tiny one, no bigger than my thumb! I'd be so happy. And we would love him with all our hearts!"

A year later, the woman gave birth to a child. He was perfectly formed but no bigger than a thumb, so the woodcutter and his wife called him Tom Thumb!

The years went by. Tom Thumb had all his parents' love and all he could wish for. He was so intelligent and clever that he succeeded in everything he undertook. However, he was still just as tiny as ever.

One day, the woodcutter went out to cut wood in the forest. He was very tired and said with a sigh:

"Ah! If only I had someone else to take the cart to the forest instead of me!"

"Father! I can drive the horse if you like," cried Tom Thumb.

"But you are much too small," said his father, laughing. "How can you hold the horse's reins?"

"I don't need reins," said Tom Thumb. "Put me in the horse's ear and I will guide it by talking to it."

The woodcutter put Tom Thumb into the horse's ear, from where he was able to tell the animal where to go, just as successfully as his father did with the reins.

One day, two strangers in the forest watched as the cart came to a halt at the very place where the woodcutter piled up his logs. Tom Thumb called out to his father:

"See, father, you don't need to be six feet tall to drive a horse."

The woodcutter got down from the cart, picked up his tiny son and put him on an ear of corn. When the two men saw the tiny, clever boy, they quickly realized that Tom Thumb could make them rich if they took him to the city. They asked the woodcutter to sell him to them.

"You're crazy! It's out of the question. Even for all the gold in the world, I would never part with my son," replied the woodcutter.

But Tom Thumb had heard the two men's offer, and he climbed up to his father's ear and whispered:

"Father, it's an opportunity to make some easy money. And I will be able to travel the country. Don't hesitate—sell me. I'll find my way home, don't worry!"

The woodcutter hesitated a long while, but Tom Thumb was so insistent that in the end he gave in. He negotiated a good price with the two men, then he waved goodbye to his son.

"Where do you want us to put you?" the men asked him as they set off.

"Oh! Put me on the brim of your hat," replied Tom Thumb. "I can walk about and look at the country."

One of the men carefully set Tom Thumb on his hat, and all three of them set out. When evening came, Tom Thumb said to the one carrying him:

"Put me on the ground, please."

"But you are not disturbing me. Stay there—you don't weigh any more than a bird dropping," replied the man.

"Yes, but I need to stretch my legs and I am dizzy from being perched up so high. Hurry up and let me down," replied Tom Thumb.

The man put Tom Thumb down beside the road near a field. The little lad ran off between the clods of earth before slipping into a field mouse's hole, which he had spotted from the hat brim.

"Good night, gentlemen! Go home without me!" he called at the entrance to the hole and burst out laughing.

The two men chased after him and drove a stick into the hole. But it was no use and, furious, they had to leave him. Tom Thumb was delighted to have played such a clever trick on people who had thought they could buy him so easily.

When Tom Thumb came out of his hiding place, he found an empty snail shell, which he made his home. But no sooner had he settled down for the night than he heard two robbers walk past, talking.

"How can we break into the parson's house tonight and rob him of all his gold and silver?" said one to the other.

Tom Thumb came out of his shell and offered his help:

"I would be very useful to you. I can slide in between the window bars and pass out everything you want."

The robbers quickly agreed to Tom's plan.

When they arrived at the parsonage, Tom Thumb slid inside and shouted as loud as he could to the two robbers outside:

"Ho! Ho! Do you want everything that's in here?"

The frightened robbers whispered:

"Don't shout like that! You'll wake up everyone!"

But Tom Thumb pretended not to hear them and shouted even louder:

"Come near the window and I will give you everything."

Alerted by the noise, the parson's maid jumped out of bed and hastened to the door. The two robbers ran off as fast as they could and Tom Thumb went and hid in the barn. Reassured that there was no one left, the maid went back to bed. Tom Thumb was very proud of his trick, which had sent the robbers fleeing. Smiling, he nestled into the hay and fell asleep, dreaming that he would soon see his parents again.

Early the next morning, he was still asleep when the cock crowed. He was in such a deep sleep that he did not hear the maid come into the barn to feed the animals.

She took a fork and lifted a clump of hay into the cow's manger. In the hay was Tom Thumb, still fast asleep. He woke up in the cow's mouth as she started to munch the hay.

"Poor me!" he cried. "I'm being chewed up!"

He realised at once where he was, and to avoid being crushed, he slid down into the cow's stomach. But lumps of hay kept coming down into his new hiding place, and there was no light. Soon he could neither move nor breathe.

"Get me out of here, I beg you! I'm suffocating!" cried Tom Thumb.

The maid, who was now milking the cow, heard the voice. She was so frightened that she fell off her stool and upset the milk. She ran as fast as she could to warn her master.

"Your Reverence! The cow is speaking!" she cried.

The curious parson rushed to the barn. No sooner had he set foot inside when he heard Tom Thumb shouting:

"Get me out of here, I beg you! I'm suffocating!"

The parson, thinking the cow was bewitched, had it killed. The butcher cut it up and the stomach, with Tom Thumb inside, was thrown away.

As Tom tried to make his escape, a hungry wolf pounced on the stomach and swallowed it whole.

Instead of despairing, Tom Thumb spoke to the animal from inside his stomach:

"Poor wolf! You look as if you're still very hungry! I know where you can have a treat. In my parents' house is a larder full of food. If you go through the kitchen drainpipe, no one will see you."

The wolf did not hesitate. As soon as night fell, he ran to Tom Thumb's house, and slithered up the drainpipe into the kitchen. Then he ate everything in the larder. His belly was so full that it was impossible for him to go back out the same way.

This was just what Tom Thumb had
planned. He began shouting as loudly as
he could in the wolf's stomach, meanwhile
doing a wild dance.

"Stop it!" said the animal. "You'll wake the
whole household!"

"Come on! You've enjoyed a feast," replied Tom
Thumb. "I've got the right to enjoy myself too!"

And Tom Thumb began shouting so loudly that in
the end he woke his parents. His father ran in carrying
an axe, and his mother followed with a scythe.

"Father, I'm in here, in the wolf's belly," shouted
Tom Thumb.

"God be praised!" exclaimed his parents happily.

"Our dear son has come home!"

His mother put down her scythe for fear of hurting
Tom Thumb, and his father aimed a fatal blow at the
wolf's head. With a knife and scissors, they opened
the wolf's belly and let their son out.

"We were beside ourselves with worry," said his father, clasping him to his heart.

"If you only knew what has happened to me," said Tom Thumb.

"I thought it would be easy to get home, but first I had to hide in a field mouse's hole, then in a snail shell. Then I found myself in a cow's stomach and finally in the wolf's belly. But now I promise I'll never leave you again," replied the little lad.

"And we won't be so stupid as to sell you again," exclaimed his parents as they hugged him.

So, after all his adventures, Tom Thumb came home at last to live peacefully with his parents, whom he always helped as much as he could.

THE END

This edition published in 2014 by Arcturus Publishing Limited
26/27 Bickels Yard, 151–153 Bermondsey Street,
London SE1 3HA
Copyright © 2013 Arcturus Publishing Limited
All rights reserved.

ISBN: 978-1-84858-762-5
CH002606US
Supplier 15, Date 1113, Print run 2976

Printed in China